Bilingual Books Collection

California Immigrant Alliance Project

Funded by
The California State Library

Mis deportes favoritos / My Favorite Sports

ME ENCANTA EL FÚTBOL/
I LOVE SOCCER

By Ryan Nagelhout   Traducido por Eida de la Vega

Please visit our website, www.garethstevens.com. For a free color catalog of all our high-quality books, call toll free 1-800-542-2595 or fax 1-877-542-2596.

Library of Congress Cataloging-in-Publication Data

Nagelhout, Ryan.
I love soccer = Me encanta el fútbol / by Ryan Nagelhout.
  p. cm. — (My favorite sports = Mis deportes favoritos)
Parallel title: Mis deportes favoritos
In English and Spanish.
Includes index.
ISBN 978-1-4824-0855-3 (library binding)
1. Soccer — Juvenile literature. I. Nagelhout, Ryan. II. Title.
GV943.25 N34 2015
796.334—d23

First Edition

Published in 2015 by
Gareth Stevens Publishing
111 East 14th Street, Suite 349
New York, NY 10003

Copyright © 2015 Gareth Stevens Publishing

Editor: Ryan Nagelhout
Designer: Nick Domiano
Spanish Translation: Eida de la Vega

Photo credits: Cover, p. 1 Fuse/Thinstock.com; pp. 5, 15, 23 Monkey Business Images/Shutterstock.com; pp. 7, 9, 19, 21 (soccer ball) Dan Thornberg/Shutterstock.com; pp. 7, 9, 19, 21, 24 (net) Fotokostic/Thinkstock.com; p. 11, 24 (pitch) romakoma/Shutterstock.com; p. 13, 24 (cleats) Stockbyte/Shutterstock.com; p. 17 Alexey Losevich/Shutterstock.com.

All rights reserved. No part of this book may be reproduced in any form without permission in writing from the publisher, except by a reviewer.

Printed in the United States of America

CPSIA compliance information: Batch #CS15GS: For further information contact Gareth Stevens, New York, New York at 1-800-542-2595.

Contenido

Diversión en el terreno 4
Juegos en el campo 10
¡Patea! 16
¡Pasa el balón! 18
Palabras que debes saber 24
Índice 24

Contents

Field Fun 4
Pitch Games 10
Kick It! 16
Pass the Ball! 18
Words to Know 24
Index 24

El fútbol es divertido.

Soccer is a lot of fun.

Me encanta correr.

I love to run.

Corro por todo
el terreno.

I run all over the field.

Al terreno también se le llama campo.

The field is also called a pitch.

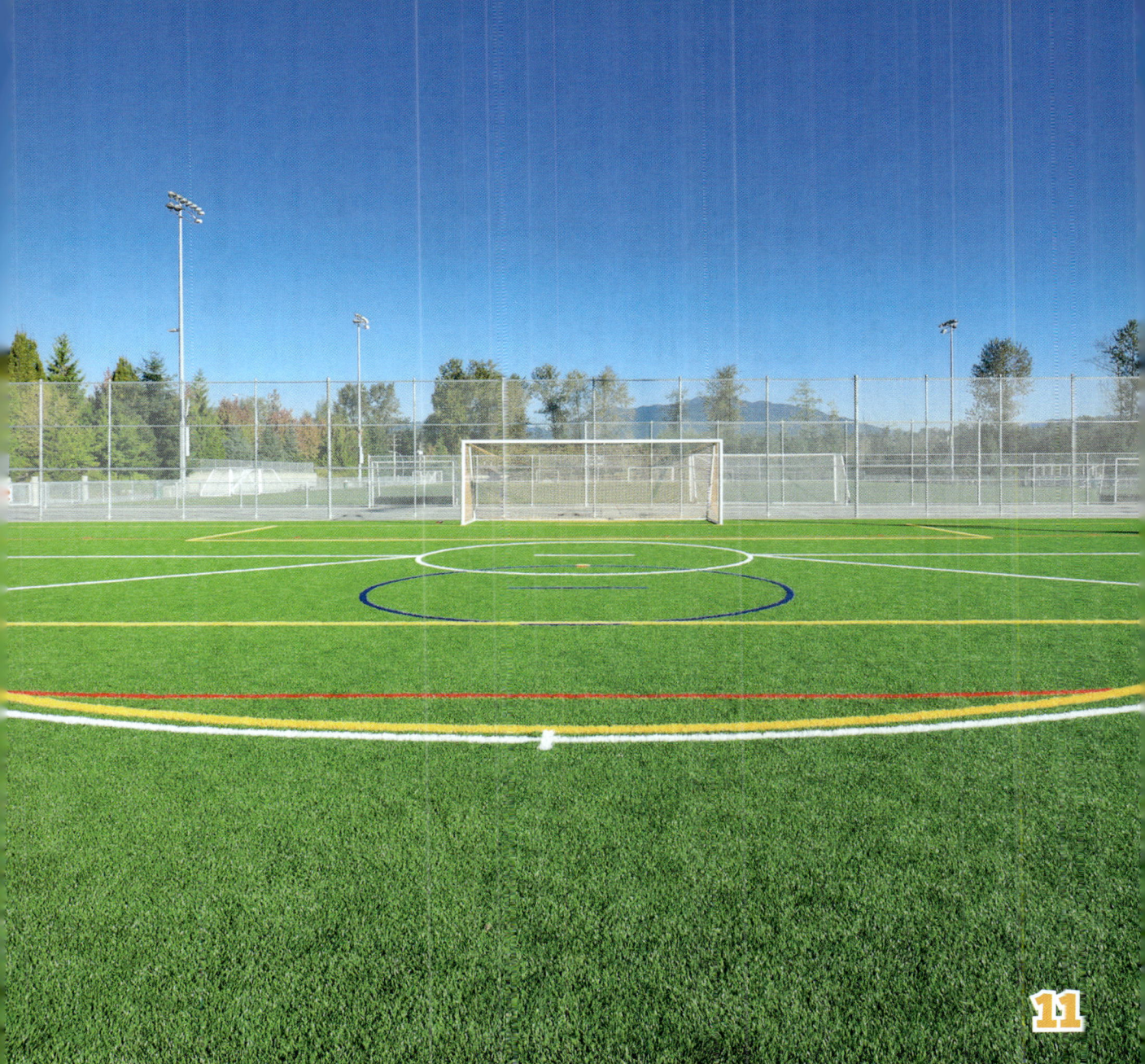

Uso botas de fútbol.
Se llaman botas
de tacos.

I wear soccer shoes.
These are called cleats.

Jugamos con un balón de fútbol. Es blanco y negro.

We play with a soccer ball. It is black and white.

Lo puedo patear lejos.

I can kick it far.

Le paso el balón
a mi amigo.

I pass the ball
to my friend.

Lo patea hacia la red.
¡Es un gol!

He kicks it into the net.
This is a goal!

¡Ven a jugar fútbol con nosotros!

Come play soccer with us!

Palabras que debes saber/ Words to Know

las botas de tacos/ cleats   la red/ net   el campo/ pitch

Índice / Index

botas de tacos/cleats 12

campo/pitch 10

gol/goal 20

red/net 20